The Celtic Mythology Collection

Other Books by Irish Imbas Books

The Beara Trilogy:
Beara: Dark Legends

The Fionn mac Cumhaill Series:
Defence of Ráth Bládhma
Traitor of Dún Baoiscne
The Adversary
Liath Luachra: The Grey One

Short Story Collections
The Irish Muse and Other Stories

The Celtic Mythology Collection 2016

Irish Imbas Books

Copyright © 2016 by Brian O'Sullivan

All rights reserved. No part of this book may be used or reproduced electronically or in print without written permission, except in the case of brief quotation.

Copyright of the stories or works in this book remains with the individual authors.

This is a work of fiction. Names, characters and incidents are products of the author's imagination or are used fictitiously and are not to be construed as real. Any resemblance to actual events, organizations or persons, living of dead, is entirely coincidental.

ISBN: 978-0-9941258-6-6

Acknowledgements

Special thanks to Marie Elder.

Table of Contents

Celtic Mythology: 1

Hawthorne Close 5

Mythological Context: Fairies 13

A Mainland Mansie Meur 19

Mythological Context: The Selkie 25

In a Small Pond 29

Mythological Context: The Salmon of Knowledge 35

Lir 39

Mythological Context: The Children of Lir 48

Transit Hours 51

Mythological Context: The Male Selkie 61

The Authors 63

The Celtic Mythology Short Story Competition 66

Another Complimentary Book 68

Other Books from Irish Imbas Books: 70

Celtic Mythology:

What we refer to as 'mythology' today was actually a framework of ideas and beliefs used by our ancestors to understand the world around them. In the absence of modern-day science and technology, these people used an approach based predominantly on observation and deduction over an extended period to make sense of the things they saw in their lives and environment but could not explain. Instead of developing theories or hypotheses to articulate those explanations as we would do today, they developed narratives or stories that used those observations and deductions. This is why so much mythology is connected to questions of creation such as 'Where did we come from?' 'Where did the moon and stars come from?' or explanations for uncommon natural phenomena such as giant waves, earthquakes, rainbows, mists and so on. These stories, and others that helped to guide how people should treat each other, formed the basis of the Celts' cultural belief system.

Since the erosion of what are generally referred to as the Celtic nations, those cultural beliefs have often been seen as something to be looked down on and many of the important cultural narratives have been classified as fantasies or relegated to the status of children's tales. As a result, despite the affection that people of Celtic heritage feel for such stories, very few actually understand them today. That lack of knowledge – the result of a great disconnect from one's cultural heritage – means that, in contemporary times, we've come to believe in skin-deep, almost cartoon-like caricatures of our own cultural origins.

Given the amount of time that's passed, it's hard to fully comprehend *how much* has been lost, even if it's easy to understand *how* it has been lost. Over the course of history, the Celtic nations were invaded and colonised by Roman, Anglo Saxon, Norman and English nations etc.). The impacts of war and domination by a foreign culture caused huge destruction of Celtic society and completely eroded the social mechanisms normally used to transfer cultural knowledge from one generation to the next. Thus the druids, the poets, the Gaelic-based educational system and the Celtic languages have fallen from favour. The scorn for Celtic culture displayed by administrative and governance systems established by the colonising cultures, combined with the increasing influence of the Christian church – an entity with a strong interest in suppressing native (and competing) belief systems – meant that the Celtic belief systems never stood a chance.

Over time, the people of the Celtic countries began to lose their stories and their language and consequently, their connection to their own history and culture. By the late 18th century, a significant proportion of cultural knowledge had already been lost. Other elements, meanwhile, were being misinterpreted and romanticised by amateur "folklorists", generally privileged writers descended from the ruling classes who had limited interaction with the native populations whose culture they were mining. No-one seemed to notice the irony that their exclusion from the established educational system meant few of the native population had the skills or opportunity to conserve their own cultural knowledge by transferring it into written form.

Fortunately, some scraps of the ancient Celtic belief systems managed to survive through the work of passionate historians and scholars who recorded and saved what knowledge they could, often at great risk to their own lives. A certain, limited, transfer of cultural narratives also continued through the ragged remnants of the last remaining poets and bards before they too died out. As a result of the efforts of these early scholars and the dedicated analysis of the information they managed to save, talented academics have managed to piece together much of that ancient knowledge over the last hundred and fifty years or so. Unfortunately, little of that work has seeped beyond the realms of academia and back out to a wider audience. In the age of the internet, where anyone can publish unsubstantiated opinions and articles that receive no peer review, cultural misinterpretation and misinformation on Celtic cultures continues to flourish.

This collection of stories by contemporary authors is a first attempt to haul Celtic stories and beliefs back out of the shadows. Love stories, action or mystery, these fascinating tales and their associated contextual contexts mark what we would like to believe is a new wave of more authentic Celtic writing. It is, we hope, a small but important first step in countering centuries of misinformation and allowing a better understanding of Celtic culture today.

Brian O'Sullivan (Wellington, 2016)

Hawthorne Close

Sighle Meehan

A builder named McGroarty bought the field.

'I got it cheap,' he told his wife.

'Because of the thorn tree?' she asked.

McGroarty laughed, poured himself a brandy. He leaned back into the good life, the pale-grey leather recliner, the classical music he was beginning to love, the artworks, the fifty-inch screen. He was well pleased with his purchase.

'It's not zoned for residential,' he admitted.

'You'll have no luck if you cut down that tree,' his wife warned.

'Arra, old wives' tales,' he said. 'What can happen?'

'Bad luck! Bad luck will follow you from the day you cut it down. It's a fairy tree.'

'You and your *piseogs*!' he teased. 'I am more than a match for any fairy I know!'

'It's where they gather,' she insisted, ignoring the innuendo. 'You will make them angry and they will work their magic on you.'

'The only magic nowadays is money,' he retorted. 'I know people in the planning department, I know people on the County Council and I know that, sooner or later, money talks.'

Sure enough, within two years the machinery was in, the field was cleared, sites were mapped and McGroarty was on the pig's back.

'Four houses,' his wife exclaimed, 'I thought you wanted six?'

'Naw! I applied for six, knowing I would be lucky to get four.'

'Are you satisfied so?'

'When am I ever satisfied!'

He speculated gleefully. There would be a tidy profit on four houses. Even three, which he had half expected, would have made a fair few bob. It was a prime location: twenty minutes drive from the city, sea views, a beach close by.

'I'm thinking of using an architect.'

'What happened to your 'natural eye for design'? I heard you say often enough you were better than any architect,' she teased.

'I am too. All those fellas with their letters and their degrees and they wouldn't know a hall from a horse's bollicks,' he grinned. 'All the same, these are great sites. An architect might be a good investment.'

McGroarty wasn't by nature honest, but he knew the importance of reputation. Sometimes he took the odd short cut but, by and large, his houses were sturdy, well built. He also knew his trade. He had trained as a carpenter but, after years in the business, he knew the intricacies of plumbing, electricals, bricklaying, plastering. He employed a young architect, struggling, but already earning a reputation for brilliance. The houses were modern, spacious, full of light. They all sold from the drawings.

He named the place Hawthorne Close even though the tree was gone and McGroarty had no idea what a close was. But he liked the sound of it.

'It has an upmarket ring, sort of English,' he told his wife.

The new owners were young couples with school-going children. They were all upgrading. Their previous houses had been too far out or too small or on the wrong side of town. They were all excited. They moved in at the start of summer and soon gardens were being planted, BBQs were being lit, friendships developing. The Hogans delivered on a promise to their children and got a puppy. But the puppy didn't thrive and died after a few weeks.

McGroarty thought of retiring. He had made a lot of money from building and it would be nice to travel. But a site came up, a spectacular site, big enough to build an entire complex of town houses. Two or three other builders had looked at it with a view to forming a syndicate but McGroarty mortgaged himself to the hilt, borrowed from his in-laws and bought the lot.

The mould appeared in the first month. The Stewarts noticed it in their kitchen on a Tuesday morning as everyone was rushing off to school or work. By evening it had spread. Vonnie Stewart wiped it off, applying bleach carefully as she didn't want to spoil the paintwork. Next evening it was worse. This time she used undiluted bleach but by the weekend it was as bad as ever.

'I'll see to it,' Reggie, her husband, said. 'It's only a mould, it can't be that difficult to treat.'

He bought pesticide, read the directions carefully, and treated a large area of wall. The mould came back. Reggie called to the Hogans, talked rugby, motor bikes.

'Any problem with mould?' he asked casually.

'Nothing much,' George Hogan replied. 'The wife doesn't use the extractor properly. I tell her she's making the kitchen damp but you know women, they never listen.' Reggie thought Betty was about to say something but her husband looked at her and she turned away.

McGroarty had a look, cursed some non-national he had used to help with the plastering.

'I'll strip that wall, treat the problem, and re-paint,' he reassured them. 'If needs be, I'll re-plaster, but that's unlikely.'

He wasn't unduly worried.

'Sorry for the inconvenience,' he added. 'I'll keep it to a minimum.'

Some weeks after the repairs were finished he received an email from Stewart. The mould was reappearing. These days McGroarty wore silk and cashmere, drove around in his merc, left the physical slog to others. But he wasn't afraid of hard work. He donned his overalls, pinned up his sleeves, and set to. He drilled, excavated, removed exterior doors and windows. He inspected wiring, pipes, disposals, searched for ingress of water.

'I'm at a loss,' he confided to his wife. 'The house is structurally sound. It's a puzzle.'

His wife said nothing, shrugged her shoulders.

He called in experts, listened to their suggestions.

'It's an unusual mould,' one man said. 'I've never seen anything like it. We could try blazing it with a cocktail of chemicals.'

For a time this seemed to work and McGroarty thought the problem was solved.

'The Mannings have their house up for sale,' Reggie Stewart announced to Vonnie one evening. 'Mould!' he added. 'Hogan told me.'

'That man,' she exclaimed. 'He knows everything. I swear I saw him looking in our windows.'

'You did,' Reggie answered. 'He looked in the windows of all the houses. They all have mould.'

'I think the children are allergic to it,' Vonnie said, listening to her eldest wheezing. 'You could be right,' Reggie agreed. 'The Hogans all have coughs. And the Manning children weren't at school this week.'

'How do you –' Vonnie started to say.

'Hogan told me,' Reggie smiled, 'he saw them through the window.'

September brought an Indian Summer. Warm, sunny days: picnics on the beach, dinners al fresco on the sheltered patios. Idyllic days for the residents of Hawthorne Close. The mould seemed to have reached a truce; it hadn't cleared but it hadn't got any worse. Wasps were the only problem, darting everywhere, more numerous and more angry than in other years.

'Shouldn't you be doing that in the spring?' James Harper observed to Reggie one evening as he passed his gate and saw Reggie busy with the secateurs.

'I'm new to gardening,' Reggie admitted. 'I am going by the book. Some shrubs can take a bit of pruning in October.'

'It's getting chilly,' James said, 'we'll soon be in the winter woolies.'

'We were spoiled by the gorgeous September,' Reggie answered. 'It was warmer outside than inside.'

'It's still warmer outside, despite the chill. Our house is very cold,' James confided.

'Have you the heating on?' Reggie asked.

'It's been on all this past week. Doesn't seem to make much difference.'

'Now that you say it, I hear Vonnie complaining about the cold,' Reggie admitted.

Six weeks later the four families held a meeting. McGroarty was to come but at the last moment he sent his apologies.

'He should be here,' Heff Manning said angrily. 'Our houses are cold. I think it is coming from that stuff on the walls.'

The mould was now a major problem, a grey-blue fungus that grew in tufts.

'It must be the foundations,' Hogan said. 'It's only on the downstairs walls.'

'It has a rotting smell,' Vonnie Stewart said. 'Like something decomposing.'

'It smells like death,' Angie Harper agreed.

'We had to…' Betty Hogan began but her husband glared at her and she didn't continue.

'Our house is freezing,' Jenny Manning complained. 'We have the heating on as high as possible and we are still shivering.

'The cold seems to come from the walls,' Reggie said. 'I think whatever is causing the mould is causing the cold.'

'We had …' Betty said.

Her husband glared at her again but she was crying now and kept going.

'We had to pull up the floorboards, they were buckling.'

'Nonsense,' Jenny argued. 'They are solid oak, they can't buckle.'

'We pulled them up,' Betty wept. 'There was mould underneath, great clumps of growth.'

'Mould isn't that strong,' Reggie protested uncertainly.

'I warned you to keep your mouth shut,' George Hogan snarled at his wife. 'We can't let this get out,' he said aggressively to the others. 'It will devalue our houses.'

'It's too late,' Jenny Manning said. 'We put our house on the market. We didn't get one bid.'

'We pitched the reserve too high,' Heff said, forcing a smile.

'No,' Jenny said. 'We have to be truthful here. We reduced the reserve, reduced it again. It made no difference. People are talking.'

'We have put every cent we own into this house,' George Hogan whispered.

Betty snuffled into a wet tissue. 'I hate this house,' she gulped. 'I wish we had never left our cosy terrace.'

'I sort of agree with you,' Vonnie said. 'But I think it's the house that hates me.'

'That's rubbish talk,' Jennie snapped. 'Houses can't hate.'

'I feel it too,' Angie Harper nodded. 'Something in the house, something hostile.'

The Mannings were older than the others, their children finishing secondary school, one already at university.

'We need a solicitor', Heff told the meeting. 'This problem won't be fixed. We must try to get our money back.'

'A court case will take ages,' Reggie groaned. 'And meanwhile the growth will mushroom. Our houses will be destroyed.'

'And maybe we won't get our money back,' Harper's face was grey. 'Barristers are slippery.'

'We will have to get something back,' George Hogan said. 'Won't we?' he pleaded.

'Our best chance is to stick together. Now I suggest,' Heff began.

'You weren't that keen on sticking together when you tried to sell your house,' Hogan accused.

'We were just testing the market, getting an idea …'

'Without a word to anyone!'

'Getting an idea on the value …'

'Look, we all know you tried to pull a fast one.' George's face was red, angry.

'Calm down, man, you will give yourself a heart attack,' Heff said smoothly.

'What do you know about this mould? What do you know that the rest of us don't? What are you not telling us?' George was on his feet, shouting at Heff.

The problem was never solved. McGroarty fought with the families, the families fought among themselves. Court cases dragged on for years. The families left, their houses unsold. Copper piping was stolen, slates disappeared, and a slimy growth pushed out in angry bursts. Squatters came and went; none stayed for more than a day or two, driven away by the deadly cold. McGroarty's drawings for his planned complex faded on his desk, his reputation shredded. He tried to sell the land but prospective buyers drove a hard bargain, knowing how badly he needed the money. He wanted to start again but his wife left him, went back to her family, and the money dried up. The banks foreclosed and he was declared bankrupt. He tried to get a job on a building site but employers were reluctant to hire him. He went on the dole, moved into a communal bed-sit.

Everyone has a different story about what went wrong in Hawthorne Close. They say McGroarty skimped on the foundations. They say he was in cahoots with cross-border smugglers and used substandard materials. There were rumours that he was too fond of high living, that he had a drink problem. Some people say the families didn't pay in full, that they left McGroarty short, that it wasn't his fault. And one or two muttered about a thorn tree but those people were elderly, rural and always muttering something daft.

Mythological Context: Fairies

Ever since I was a kid in West Cork, I've been wary of 'fairies'. Down in Beara, we had an old neighbour called Thady who claimed to see strange lights up on the hill at night. On those nights, he told us, the fairies would come to torment him, causing strange noises up on his roof or knocking on his door after midnight. Thady lived quite far up the road from us, an isolated *botharín* (little road) that led down to the sea. It was a lonely spot and although there were at least four other houses on that road, all of them were empty and in various states of disrepair. Two were in ruins, two others had been deserted by families who'd died out or moved overseas. It truly was an isolated spot and that isolation did nothing to help him overcome his fear of 'fairies'.

Over toward Ballydehobb, I also knew an old woman who claimed her house had been built on an old *Sidhe* path – a kind of unmapped path where the 'fairies' are said to travel. Not far from where she lived, there was an old blackthorn tree that she insisted was their favourite place to gather. There were also several old *ráth* up and down the coast – what people now often call 'fairy forts' – where mothers warned their children not to tread. In fact a *ráth* is just the ruin of an ancient farming settlement and has nothing to do with 'fairies' but removed from their cultural history over the centuries, people had to find some rationale to explain the existence of these substantial old structures. In that regard, the 'fairies' fit the bill perfectly.

As I grew older and became more informed, I learned some odd things about Irish 'fairies'. I was surprised to find, for example, that the word 'fairy' was actually an Anglicization of an old continental European word. Despite what I'd been told at school it wasn't a direct translation for *'Na Sidhe'* or the *'Tuatha Dé Danann'*. In fact, 'the fairies' bore no meaningful resemblance to those Otherworld figures referred to throughout the ancient Irish manuscripts.

The first thing you should know is that when you're referring to creatures of Celtic mythology, it's probably more correct to avoid the word 'fairy' completely. The namby-pamby, flower-hoppers with wings that adorn the Enid-Blyton books of old were never truly part of Celtic mythology. In particular, when talking about Irish/Scottish mythological creatures – essentially the same things – it's always better to use the Gaelic term '*sí*' or '*sith*' (pronounced 'shee') or '*síog*' or – in plural form – '*Na Sidhe*' or '*Na síoga*'. [The Welsh too had specific terms that corresponded to the English word but as I have no expertise on this topic, I've not discussed them here.]

The word '*sí*' is derived from an ancient Celtic word '*síd*' which was the name for the giant mounds that held tumuli or passage graves where some of our far-distant ancestors were buried. This is why *Na Sidhe* – until the last century or two – were often portrayed as, or confused with, representations of the dead.

In pre-historic and pre-medieval Ireland, it seems certain that *Na Sidhe* were usually understood to be a kind of mirror image of humanity. In the oldest manuscripts, they are described as looking like us, speaking like us and, in general, acting like us, displaying all the character traits, both positive and negative, we'd associate with typical human behaviour. The two key aspects that differentiated *Na Sidhe* from their human counterparts however, were that they (a) lived in the Otherworld and (b) had access to exclusive knowledge and powers.

In much of the surviving pre-medieval literature, when *Na Sidhe* interacted with humans they were generally portrayed doing so as equals, if not superiors. They were never, ever, 'little people'.

As the Celtic nations were invaded and conquered, their cultural belief systems were also eroded, which disrupted the transfer of traditional knowledge about *Na Sidhe/Tuath Dé Danann*. This transfer process was further disrupted by events such as the Great Famine in Ireland, the Clearances in Scotland and the exacerbated weakening of Celtic languages as native speakers died or immigrated in great numbers. Oppressed on all sides, over time *Na Sidhe* also took on an increasingly derivative form, shrinking (metaphorically and descriptively) in the stories they inhabited. Much of the stories with negative connotations associated with them also developed over this period as the Church asserted its position that belief in such entities was unacceptable competition at best, outright evil at worst.

Ironically, while knowledge of Celtic mythological figures was diminishing in the Celtic nations, reduced expressions of what they'd represented began to flourish in England under a new name: fairies. Distorted versions of the old Celtic mythological figures had been appearing in medieval romances, initially as Otherworldy enemies to the (mostly Christian) protagonists but, in later centuries, taking on a more alluring and less menacing role. In this new, sanitised form, the 'fairies' started turning up in literature such as Edmund Spenser's *'Faerie Queen'*, Shakespeare's *'A Midsummer Night's Dream'* and many others. Much later, during the Romantic Period (at its peak from around 1800 to 1850) when older cultural tropes were mined for inspiration purposes, the use of 'fairies' became even more popular.

The famous 1920 Strand Magazine article with the photos of the 'Cottingley Fairies' changed the visual portrayal of the earlier mythological creatures forever. From that point on, the word 'fairies' came to mean tiny, winged creatures who hid away in nature's quiet places but who also retained a tantalising whiff of mystery and magic. Following that Strand article, the associated visual imagery became prettier and the 'fairy' figures drifted further and further from the mythological sources from which they'd been derived (aided in no small part by the famous 'flower fairies' pictures produced by Cicely Mary Barker and others). Over the latter part of the twentieth century, those became the images of 'fairies' that most people became familiar with. By then, of course, they were little more than a fantasy fabrication that had very little to do with Celtic mythology and had incorporated elements not only of 'Ye Olde English folklore' but of Germanic elves, classical Romano-Greek nymphs and satyrs, a mish-mash of Tolkien imagery and of course Disney's plastic, sugar-coated Tinkerbell.

Back in Ireland and Scotland meanwhile, detached from their original interpretation, the *Sidhe/ Tuatha Dé Danann* were gradually replaced by a diminutive new interpretation (the *síoga*) created from a merging of the remnants of the original beliefs, the dominant church teachings and the English-based 'fairy'. As the Gaelic languages were killed off, even the term *síoga* was increasingly replaced by the English term.

Over the late nineteenth and early twentieth century, these fairies came to represent an invisible source of mischief and malevolent purpose. In rural areas, they were held responsible for evil happenings and very much embodied the precarious balance of life in isolated agricultural communities. These particular 'fairies' stole babies and replaced them with changelings. They tainted the milk and butter and required offerings to appease them. They wrought disaster on individuals who disturbed their infrastructure; their *ráth*, their paths and their thorn bushes. It was on the coat-tails of this interpretation of 'fairies' that I and many of my contemporaries grew up, although by then it had already been irreversibly diminished by the availability of electricity, education and the influences of television.

Hawthorne Close almost perfectly epitomises the fairy folklore in Ireland and Scotland that most people above the age of thirty to forty will be familiar with. By focussing her story on the physical consequences of crossing the fairies rather than on the fairies themselves, Sighle Meehan gets straight to the heart of twentieth century 'fairy' lore. These 'fairies' represented the 'dangerous unseen', the things we don't fully believe but don't fully disbelieve either. In her story, they remain silent and unseen, off to the side and out of sight. And they're all the more dangerous for that. Had they been described in full, as in the Ireland and Scotland of the fifties, sixties and seventies when technology and science dragged 'fairy' lore into the light of day, their potency would have been extinguished.

[Additional Note: In more recent times, the interpretation of 'fairies' appears to have morphed once more, homogenised in the great 'melting pot' of international travel and communication where elements of different cultures are reduced to nonsensical meaning. Over the last two decades, 'fairies' have been increasingly restricted to the female gender and transformed to a kind of sexualised, elf-like form (complete with pointed ears, short skirts and a pout). This particular theory can be verified or disproved by merely entering the internet search term 'fairy image'.].

Brian O'Sullivan

A Mainland Mansie Meur

Sheelagh Russell-Brown

There's Orkney tales of spirit babes that haunt the unholy earth where they are buried. Around their graves, white birds fly up just after sunset, and strange lights in the sky are seen at night.

Except when we have lightning, though. Storm lightning like we have now. Or when I spot a whitemaa [a seagull] that's lost its path. There's no such uncanny doings here along the Saint John River, far from the white and empty shores of Sanday. I know the spot where lie our babes is sacred earth, and our babes no unbaptized children. It's calm and peaceful there and that is why we're drawn, though on our own, not we two together.

At times I swear I have a Selkie bride and I a mainland Mansie Meur. Effie's long saved me from drowning but now she tends her remaining young, jealous and flegged my attentions will put in peril all that's left. At times she slips from me like the old tale Selkie slipped from Mansie Meur. She's like the peedie mother jay, dancing and chattering when I'm at my building, luring me away from the nest of chicks hidden in the pines.

And some days, when my Effie thinks that I'm not noticing, I see her pick some Black-Eyed Susans, some snowdrops and some campions as our wee Janet loved, to carry to their graves by the furthest apple tree. Effie could not bear to have them taken from her and buried in the churchyard, no matter that it was the English church.

And all about us are the woods. These woods, they smother me. They say to me that they belong, that they were here before I came, before I and all the others came. And will be here long after.

The Micmac ['Mi'kmaq: First Nation tribe], they live among them, taking what they need in sap and in bark for their canoes, in branches for their fires, in meat for their suppers. But the Micmac let the forests live and they return the favour. They have their stories too, stories that grow from this, their land.

As I have mine.

The trees push back against us here, us who don't belong. They'd bury us if they could. With our own stories, then, we'll have back the clean and grassy land of home, the open shore. No more the lichen-crusted stones, the stony soil, the soiled hands — hands now fighting to repel the crowd of trees that o'errun this savage space.

But some trees I've taken out. I must build here a better home, although my heart's home is Sanday's shores. And here therefore, I sing my songs and tell my stories. For folks need songs, they need such stories. Without the tales we build and tell, we've naught to put our needs and natures to, naught to hold us back from being lost.

But now the storm has passed us by, the lightning to the south dimming. Yet still we sit in our small shelter aneath the stairs till Effie's satisfied the danger's gone. And, so, it's time for stories.

Effie's stories are full of horror, of demon lovers and cut-off hands, like them her father must have heard from a mother raised on Russian steppes. She's mainland raised, Effie. At home here with the haunted woods where I am not. She has a book of Pushkin that she brought with her upon our marriage, and from it she has read me of his tales and songs. These tales I'd never tell to my own children, no matter that she says Pushkin learned them at his nurse's knee. What sort of nurse this Russian must have had! Effie gives the children horrors enough with her own flegging about the bats, the lightning, and the poison vapours in the woods.

Instead, I tell the story of Mansie Meur and the Selkie who never forgot. His name is our own family name – the Orkney Meur, the English Muir – and that always tickles them. When Mansie wants to steal the seal pups from their mother and use their pelts to make a weskit [waistcoat], I make the mother's beerin' moan, and the children clap their hands. I tell it them in Norn, the tongue of my forefathers, for it's a part I do not want for them to lose. And I've lost enough already. I tell it here in English though, at least in those words that I know.

'Mansie Meur, he was a limpet gatherer and it was a hard, poor life for him. He had no wife nor children for he could not build a home or feed them. Instead he bent on slippery rocks, and as he picked the limpets up and put them in the basket, their weight it bent a crook'd back still further, He dreamed of living in a fine house like that the rulers once had on his small island. He dreamed of silk and furs instead of rough woollen trews and weskit that held the water.

One day at work as he was dreaming — a grey and drizzly day, much like every other—he heard a keening beyond the rocks where he was standing and saw a Selkie with sleek black fur and handsome eyes, with lashes fine and long like fairy's webs — much like your mother's eyes in fact. And there were tears caught in the corners, for she was giving birth—'

At this, my Effie gives me a kick and such a look! I know that look. It's warning me that such stories can birth questions parents daren't answer yet. But they've heard this tale so many times before that I just hurry on. Mayhap some day when they are older, such unwanted questions will follow.

'As Mansie sits and watches from a stone above the ocean, he sees twin baby Selkies appear — perhaps a boy and girl like you two here. And then he has a thought, sudden-like. Baby Selkie coats, so fresh and clean, would make for him a fine weskit and with such riches close at hand who knows but that a fine house might follow. And if he had the mother too? Perhaps a hat to crown his head.

He makes a grab and takes the kittens that wriggle in his arms then settle in to suckle at his buttons while their poor mother – faster – slips away.

But then he hears her gurn and cry and looks towards the rocks beyond. The Selkie wife now with her Selkie man. She turns her head and gives poor Mansie such a look. There's water in the corners of her eyes for she is weeping. And Mansie, he cannot be so cruel to take them babies from their Ma. And so he puts them on the skerry and their mother goes to them and keeps them close.

So Mansie never did get his fine weskit and kingly hat, but he worked on and one day he was married with babes of his own that he too kept close.'

With this I steal a look at Effie, bent over her mending so I cannot see the tears in her fine eyes. Her hair is black and sleek like Selkie's hair, with still no touch of grey. I would that I were more like Mansie Meur and give her back her young ones once again. But still there's two that we've been left, who clap their hands for they know the rest from many tellings.

'One day, young Mansie — now not so young — and bent and burdened with care of his small family, must leave to look for fish along the shore. He stands upon a rock and brings in fish after fish, some for that day's meal and many more to cure and smoke for winter days ahead.

But he's been careless, dreaming still of riches that may come, and soon enough the tide is all about his fishing rock and he cannot reach the land. He looks about but the shore is empty — much like these woods if someone strays from the path.'

— a little warning's not to go amiss. We've lost too much already, my Selkie bride and I, her mainland Mansie.

'A Selkie weskit might keep the cold water from his skin if had one, but naught can stop the water creeping up his body. He tastes its saltiness and coughs it out loudly.'

And here I cough and loll about to make the babies laugh, for they've never tasted the salt sea here, so far away from the ocean's shore.

'And so he says goodbye to wife and babes, and then, just then — what happens?'

The children gasp though they have heard this many times.

Just then he feels a wee tug on his collar and looks around to see the Selkie's eyes, now filled with tears, not with flegging for her little ones but for the little limpet gatherer who'd not taken them. The Selkie's coat is grey now, her eyes a little dim, but still she tugs and tugs and soon wee Mansie finds his feet can touch the shingle. And then he looks behind and what do you suppose?

The wee ones clap their hands again.

'The Selkie returns to Mansie's flooded stone and brings back to him his fishing creel in her now toothless mouth. 'And Mansie Meur, he said to himself—'

The children clap their hands again and shout together, 'Geud bliss the selkie that deus no' forget'!'

I see that Effie wishes the story to be in the Queen's own English, and I've done what she wants, but such a tale needs its own words to tell it, not those of a foreign ruler.

Every time I tell the tale, I cannot put out of mind how the loss of two young ones is more than just a tale, how no amount of beering or tears will bring them back to Effie and me. If only there'd been such a Selkie the day that Tommy drowned. But the hope that no good deed goes unrewarded comforts our wee children, they who have no memories of a brother and a sister lost to trouble them. I hope it comforts Effie, too.

I watch their tiny heads nod and drop and we carry them to bed.

When Effie's not looking, I find my steps have carried me to talk to my now-gone peedies, my little ones, my first-born son and daughter. 'My Tommy boy, I'll build a boat and ye shall sail it, just like the paper boats we'd build together. Ye'll be with me, I know, when I'm out upon the water.'

'And Janet. My sma' and gentle Janet, we'll bring you too. Your voice and gentle ways could tame the Tangie, all covered with his kelp, and bring us safely back to harbour.'

And yet we two, Effie and I, we cannot mourn together. Instead we get on as best we can with our building of what we think will rescue us. Although the apples from that tree beside the graves grow thick and heavy, we cannot bring ourselves to pick them. Instead they fall, all in a rookel upon the ground, feeding the wasps and creepi-craalies. No good can come to us from such a harvest.

The harvest from the earth and other trees I gather grudgingly, but I gather. Our small remaining family have need of what this land gives up. Yet it has taken from us what cannot be given back. The stony pool that claimed my son, the pestilent air that filled my daughter's lungs, the snow that clarted up my path when I went after help – I hate them. As I hate the choice that brought us here, and I the one that made it.

Now what can I do but build, give them a house like Mansie dreamed of, take only what I have to of the devil's store.

Build what I must to save us.

Mythological Context: The Selkie

Due to the close association between water and the spiritual world in ancient times, the Otherworld was often considered to be located underwater (usually in the sea but also accessible through lakes and rivers) and there are numerous old stories and folklore associated with this belief. It's no surprise therefore, that a number of narratives subsequently came into being involving creatures who lived underwater (the *maighdean marra* [mermaid] and *fear mara* [merman]) but who behaved and operated within the established constraints of '*Na Sidhe*', that is, linked to the dead and potentially dangerous to humans.

These underwater creatures were very different to the more contemporary interpretation of what's commonly known as the mermaid: a creature with a human torso and a fish-like tail. The latter are based on elements from Assyrian tales, the Greek sirens and other, later, influential narratives such as Hans Christian Andersen's 'The Little Mermaid'. Elements of these overseas stories did enter Ireland, Scotland and Wales from medieval times and are thought to have had some influence on the portrayal of the original Celtic mythological creatures.

One of the most common stories involving the *maighdean mara* tells of a young man who spots a beautiful woman on the sea shore. When the woman puts her magic cloak aside, the man seizes it, thus taking her under his power. Accompanying him home, the *maighdean mara* becomes his wife and they have a number of children. One day, one of those children discovers the magic cloak (which had been hidden by the young man) and returns it to his mother. Taking the cloak, she flees back to the sea and enters it, never to be seen again. Variations of this legend are believed to have spread to Scotland and Iceland in the late Middle Ages.

Up in the Orkney islands and the Western Isles of Scotland, these stories appear to have developed into a more specialised lore around a seal people called Selkie (the word 'selkie' is thought to be an old Orcadian dialect for "grey seal") although those tales are also found in other parts of Scotland and Ireland. Much of the more common lore with respect to selkie seems to have been sourced specifically from the works of a nineteenth century Orkney writer, Walter Traill Dennison, who wrote a number of tales based on beliefs and traditions from that area, many of them romanticised and possibly differing from the original lore through the transfer to prose. The most prominent theme to this selkie folklore relates to their shapechanging ability: they are seals who can take on human form by removing their skin or pelt. If that skin is lost or taken, the selkie is restricted to human form until it is recovered.

Sheelagh Russell Brown's use of the old tale "The Selkie that deud no' Forget", originally published by the Walter Traill Dennison in 1880, is a classic and effective use of a 'tale within a tale', in this case providing a brilliant foil to grief-stricken parents to heart-breaking effect.

Brian O'Sullivan

In a Small Pond

Marc McEntegart

Around sunset, the boy would come to find the old man fishing in the pool, the day's catch lying in the cool black earth of its bank. The boy would gather up the fish and the two would make their way back to the tumbledown cottage. There, they would eat the fish while the aging poet Finnegas taught the boy Fionn as best he could.

The two spent their daytime hours apart, the boy tending to the house and occasionally snaring a rabbit, while the poet continued his quest for knowledge. By night, Finnegas would sing him the old poems and Fionn would ask questions about the world around them.

Though she had never seen these things, she knew them to be true, because she knew all there was to know.

When they had first met, the poet had refused to take Fionn in, his days being full already with his fishing in the hope of ultimate wisdom. Indeed, the two had met in the poet's house and its state of sorry disarray was evident from the loose sheafs of paper littering every available surface. The old man would have turned him away, had the boy not offered to guarantee the smooth running of his home in exchange for an education. They shook on it over the yellowing pages of some abandoned verse, and Fionn agreed to facilitate the old man's quest for the salmon of knowledge.

As their months together became years, Fionn's mind sharpened. From time to time, he would ask questions that the sagely poet could not answer. At first, they were the simple and direct questions that only a child would think to ask, but as he grew he would pose problems to which the poet could not put his mind. In those cases, Finnegas would smile and make a note of the boy's question, sure that the day would come when he would answer them all.

Once, the boy had watched him add a question to the stack of unanswerables and asked, 'And how do you know the salmon of knowledge is real?'

The poet gave him a sympathetic look and said, 'I wouldn't believe it if I hadn't seen him myself, boy, large as life.'

She knew this, because she knew all there was to know.

Isolated from the flow of the river proper, she had circled her pool for long years without change. The sun would slide across the sky each day, the moon each night, and by and by the seasons would pass. Summers would give way to autumns with red-brown leaves drifting on the water's surface, until the first freeze of winter pinned them in place. The darkness of winter would give way to the lightness of summer like night to day.

With the weight of her accumulated wisdom came the understanding that, as long as she lived, she would remain in her pool by the Boyne. For her, there would be no long, against-the-current struggle to where she was spawned. She would lay no eggs before she died, she would have no successor. The world would know only one salmon of knowledge.

When the poet first arrived, she had found him a tremendous novelty. She would wait each morning to see him approach, his silhouette a welcome change among the reeds that surrounded her pool. Before long, though, he had become just another part of the too-familiar pattern. Just before dawn each morning, his lure would appear on the water, and she would watch it as it twitched above the pool.

As the sun rose, its light would touch the lure before it reached into the water. For a few short seconds, that twist of shining feathers suspended just on the surface was seductive even to her. Many fish had snapped at it only to find themselves snagged, tugged struggling from the safety of the pool.

She knew that she would one day follow them.

She knew too that, each morning, Finnegas would watch her while she eyed the lure, his eyes as round and unblinking as her own. He'd watch until the sunlight pierced the pool, when she'd twist and disappear into the depths, the morning sunshine gleaming along her flank. That momentary sheen of sun on scale was her lure, her guarantee that he would come back the following day.

Though he had been young and strong when his search for ultimate wisdom began, she had watched grey creep into his hair and a bend make its way up his back. She had watched his skin tan and crack over long years in the elements. Where once he had stood tall and proud, he had been eaten away by his hunger for her. He had confined himself for too long to this short stretch of the Boyne.

She knew enough of the world to know that her wisdom would die with him on the banks of the Boyne. He would continue to compose poetry, and sing it to any who happened upon him, but he would do so alone. For all the wisdom in the world, Finnegas would father no children, would have no successor. He could no more leave his pool than she could hers.

But even the boy Fionn would leave him one day, and in that there was the hope that some part of her might survive to see something more than the same rock and water, the same sunrises and seasons. At length, she began to form a plan, for even with all the knowledge in the world a salmon is not naturally inclined to planning. Her plan would require her to wait until the day was right. She would need it to be cold for the old man to leave the boy alone while the she cooked.

Everything would need to be just so, but she had time, she had waited before and she would know when the time was right.

It happened on a crisp November morning, the sun cool and hugging the horizon, the first freeze of the season just visible at the top of her pool. The sunshine highlighted the soft edges of the ice at the banks as she stared up at the lure and knew that today would be the day that she would bite. The lure filled her vision as she breached the surface, the brilliant yellow of its feather not quite covering the gleam of the hook.

The old poet carried his prize home held high over his head, the salmon still wriggling as he carried it aloft, an instinct that all the knowledge in the world could not smother. When he returned to the tiny cottage he shared with the boy, Fionn was sweeping the floor. At the sound of the door, he looked up to see Finnegas triumphant, the enormous fish held aloft.

'Stoke the fire, lad. Today's the day.'

The boy set to work as Finnegas gutted the fish, stacking more firewood on the hearth and setting the spit in place. When the old poet was done, his hands trembling, he set the fish on the spit and looked his student in the eye, 'Fionn, winter's closing in and it looks like being a long day, we'll need more firewood. For all the care I've given you, promise me you won't eat any part of this salmon before I return.'

The boy gave a solemn nod. After his master had left, he turned the spit steadily until the fish began to crackle. Obedient to a fault, he didn't flinch from his task until the skin began to crack and spit, sending a thin jet of fat onto his thumb. Reflexively, he raised it to his mouth to soothe the burn, and all at once received a flash of brilliant insight, a hundred thousand thoughts and memories came crashing in on him. He reeled as he felt the world expand around him in every direction. Numb with realisation, his left hand continued to turn the spit.

There are those who will tell you that when Finnegas returned, he saw the light of wisdom on Fionn's face, and knew immediately what had transpired. As it happened, the search for firewood took longer than expected. When the poet returned, Fionn had had the time to pull himself together. He had prepared the fish for the older man and laid it on the table, seasoned with a little salt and the few herbs that had survived into winter.

When Finnegas was ready, he sat and began to eat, and as he ate the boy sat opposite him and asked, 'Finnegas?'

'Yes?'

'If the salmon of knowledge knew all that there is to know…'

'Yes?'

'Then she knew about fishermen, knows about you…'

'Yes?'

'Why would she ever take the bait?'

Smiling, the poet chewed and stared down at his plate as he searched his mind for the answer, but his face fell as he found that he had no response for the boy. With the silence stretching between them, he realised that Fionn wasn't waiting for an answer, wasn't even looking at him. Instead, his student's eyes were fixed on the tabletop between them, an uncharacteristically morose expression on his face.

Fionn had expected the older man to be furious, but instead he seemed to sag, withering under the weight of the realisation. Shaking his head, Finnegas slid his plate across the table and bade the boy eat the remainder of the salmon. While the boy ate, Finnegas stood and walked about the room, packing the boy's few small belongings into an old leather pack. When Fionn had finished, the old man handed him the bundle and sent him out into the cool air of early evening.

With the gloom of twilight closing in and his breath misting in front of him, Fionn lifted his thumb to his mouth and once again knew all that there was to know, all there ever was, and much that might once have been. With eyes open wide and round, he inspected the few yellow-brown leaves still on the trees, plucking one and turning it this way and that.

He shut his eyes and listened to the distant gurgle and suck of the Boyne, knowing how it looked and sounded from below, how it felt to twist and turn in the water. He knew the rush of water over fins and gills, knew what it was to spend long years alone, knew how it felt to have longed to be something more.

He looked back at the cottage that he had shared with Finnegas. At the thought of him, Fionn remembered what it was like to twist and writhe in the old poet's hands, coarse fingers against his scales as he struggled for life. He knew with a chilling certainty that he would never again meet the old man.

The part of him that was still a boy pulled his thumb from his mouth. As the tide of knowledge receded, he could almost forget what it was to know all there was to know, could almost forget what it was to have been a fish, could almost forget what it was like to have spent lifetimes alone beneath the surface of a pool by the Boyne.

He felt the familiarity of the place closing in on him then, the cottage, the wind in the trees, and the pool by the river all too much, a little too close to home. He hitched up his pack and started walking. He didn't pick a direction.

He knew it wouldn't matter. He knew where he was going, because he knew all there was to know.

Mythological Context: The Salmon of Knowledge

Of all the Fenian Cycle tales, the story of Fionn and the Salmon of Knowledge has generally remained, if not the most preferred, then certainly the most well known. Believed to date from the tenth century, the earliest remaining version of the tale is found in the twelfth century text *Macgnímartha Find* (the Boyhood Deeds of Fionn). A section of that text outlines how a seven-year old Fionn, named Demne in the text, goes to the Boyne to learn the skills of a poet from the poet/druid Finnegas and the subsequent events that occur there. Marc McEntegart's version of this ancient tale is unique in that he doesn't use the perspective of Fionn or Finnegas – normally, the two principal characters – to tell the story. Instead, he focuses on the Salmon of Knowledge itself which gives those subsequent events an epic, almost timeless quality.

Tradition has it that the well of Seghais, the source of the River Boyne, was encircled by hazel trees that dropped their nuts (often used by our ancestors as a metaphor for wisdom) into the water. These floated downriver where they were eaten by a salmon that, by consuming the nuts, absorbed all the wisdom and knowledge of the hazel trees.

At heart, the Salmon of Knowledge story in the Fenian Cycle seems quite a simple one but in fact there are layers within it. The name of the poet/druid Finnegas (or Finnéices) for example, literally means 'Fionn the Seer' which is far too odd to be sheer coincidence and, possibly, refers to Fionn himself as an older and wiser man. The core theme of the story, meanwhile – a hero's acquisition of esoteric or forbidden knowledge through the consumption of magical food – is one that's found among the mythology of many different cultures. Welsh mythology has a very similar version outlined in *Historia*

Taliesin (The Tale of Taliesin) which describes how the early Brythonic poet Taliesin (Gwion Bach in the story) acquired the gift of knowledge by stealing three magic drops from Cerodwen's cauldron.

Similarly, in Norse mythology there's a version of the story where the legendary hero Sigurd, having killed a dragon, is asked by his comrade Regin to roast the dragon's heart. While Sigurd is carrying out this task, a sudden spurt of blood from the heart burns his thumb and, putting it into his mouth to cool it, he finds he's received the knowledge to understand the speech of birds. Afterwards, when he eats the dragon heart he gains the gift of 'prophesy', just as Fionn does.

If you look at one of the creation stories in the Book of Genesis, of course, you'll also find that similar pattern where Eve takes a bite out of the apple from the forbidden tree of knowledge. It just goes to show how old stories often hide many truths that go deeper than the literal ones.

Brian O'Sullivan

Lir

Coral Atkinson

You can hate me if you choose; most folk do. I'm the one that did the deed, the wicked stepmother who deserved what she got.

The storytellers and harpists spread it about that I'm dead. A convenient falsehood that discourages gossip, so I don't dispute their silly lie. No one recognises me now, or remembers that the ancient hag in the black shawl mumbling among the rocks was ever young.

Boys call me 'The Crow', but never to my face. Girls snigger when they see me coming and run when I wave my stick. 'Keep away from that old witch, she might turn you into a pig or worse,' the mothers say.

I had that knack once, not that it did me any good. Quite the reverse.

Aobh and I were sisters, daughters of Bodhbh Dearg, the Ard Rí [High King]. We had golden bells that tinkled in our curls and when we walked our hair was so long it dragged in the dew on the grass. Aobh was the elder. She had sea-blue eyes and her gowns were every shade of blue. My eyes were green and my clothes were the green of a hundred hues.

'One day a marvellous young king will come and sweep me away and marry me.'

Aobh smiled into the bronze looking-glass as she spoke.

'He might like me better,' I said, grabbing the mirror from my sister's hand.

'Why would he?' said Aobh.

'I'm younger, and prettier,' I said.

'You're covered in puppy fat.'

I stuck out my tongue and we both laughed. We had this argument many times, though both of us knew the way things were, neither of us would ever be a bride. My father gave us rare and expensive gifts, gold and silver cloak pins, circlets, and torques set with precious stones. He also kept us prisoners. We lived with our guards and Orla our old servant in a *crannóg*, on an island in the lake. We were never allowed to cross the water to the *ráth* where Bodhbh Dearg held court.

It wasn't that we lacked suitors; kings and princes swarmed in from every corner of the country to woo us, but we were forbidden to meet any of them. None was ever considered suitable in my father's eyes. One was too short, another too tall, a third too poor. We even heard of a prince who was rejected because the toes of his boots turned up.

When the right man comes, you'll thank me for my caution,' Bodhbh Dearg said.

'Couldn't we just have a peep at some of these fellows?' Aobh asked.

'Certainly not!' Bodhbh Dearg flung his cloak over one shoulder to show he tolerated no further argument. 'I'm not having my daughters running about, falling in love with any Dermot, Fintán or Brian that passes by.'

'But we're prisoners here,' I said. 'It's cold and wet, the thatch on the roof leaks and we never meet anyone or have any fun.'

My father scowled. 'At least you both are safe. I have many enemies and princesses not only need protection from the *amadáin* who might want to marry them, but also from murderers, kidnappers and those who'd gouge out your eyes.'

He pulled open the door and nodded to the boatman that he was ready to leave.

There was a storm that night. The water of the lake heaved and struggled in the darkness. The moon disappeared behind a black veil, the stars vanished and rain tumbled from the sky.

'A dirty old night,' one of the guards called to the other.

'It is that,' shouted his companion.

I snuggled down among the furs of my bed, glad I wasn't outside. The deluge grew heavier. It made sloshing, slopping noises, sounding more like the sea than the rain.

In the light of the fire I could see water creeping through the rushes on the floor. Strings of rain poured through the thatches of the roof and hit my bed.

'We're being flooded.' Aobh jumped up and I did the same. Orla went on snoring.

A surge of water hit the house, the door crashed open and the room was filled with the tang of salt and a faint bluish light. A young man stepped towards us. He was tall and fair as butter. His ringed hands moved about like pale birds and his tunic and cloak were woven in the colours of royalty. I had never seen anyone so beautiful.

Aobh gave a soft cooing noise, which made me think she felt the same. The guards stared at the astounding stranger, swords ready in their hands and gobs hanging open. They didn't move.

'Pardon, ladies, for my intrusion, but desperate times call for desperate measures. Lir, of the Ocean, at your service.' He bowed.

Aobh and I dropped curtseys. I was embarrassed at being seen by this gorgeous man in my undergarments, though the manner in which Aobh let her shift fall from one shoulder made me feel she saw it as an advantage.

Lir smiled at Aobh and winked at me. 'Like many men I am in search of a bride. I had heard of the exquisite sisters Aobh and Aiofe, so I came searching. Bodhbh Dearg is generous in his hospitality but he refused to consider me for a son-in-law or let me see his lovely daughters.

'He refuses everyone,' Aobh said.

'Did my father say why you were unsuitable?' I could feel myself blush as I spoke.

'He didn't fancy his daughter living far away and he believes the ocean is not a fitting home for a land princess.'

Lir shook his long hair and glimmering drops of water flew about.

'I have little time,' he said. 'Any moment my absence from the banquet will be noticed and I may be pursued. They say your father threatens death to any man who finds his way to this *crannóg*. I caused the little storm as a diversion so I could get through the lake unobserved.'

'You can create storms?' Aobh asked.

Lir flexed his shoulders and his multi-hued cloak swam with colour. 'At sea, I can stir a tempest, make a tidal wave or sink a ship, but here on land my powers are few. I have used up what I have of storm magic tonight, so I need to hurry.' He paused. 'But it seems I face a dilemma as to which of you should receive my proposal. You girls are so desirable. I would be happy to invite either of you to be my wife.'

Aobh and I looked at each other. I knew we both wanted to be the chosen one.

'Pick the elder,' Aobh said.

'The younger,' I added.

'No,' Lir said. 'I will seek marriage to the lady with the eyes that are nearest in colour to the blue of the ocean.'

'That's me,' Aobh squealed. 'Everyone says I have sea-blue eyes.'

There was no way I could deny it, though disappointment hit me like a cast stone. Aobh ran to Lir, caught one of his hands and looked at him intently. She was always rather forward but Lir didn't seem to mind. He stared into her eyes and immediately got down on one knee and asked her to be his wife.

'Yes, yes,' bubbled Aobh, throwing her arms around his neck.

I started to cry for I knew Lir would take Aobh away. She would be Lir's queen and I would be shut up here, lonely and sad. Aobh and I had laughed at our father's worries that we might be murdered, kidnapped, ransomed, or have our eyes put out. But these things happened and were to be feared. The threats would be worse now, faced on my own.

Lir seemed to know my thoughts. Untangling himself from Aobh's embrace, he advanced towards the fire. Stooping, he put his hand into the flames, as though oblivious to the heat. There was a loud sizzling noise and he withdrew a blackened stick.

'There is no need to fear ever again.' He handed me the stick. 'I'm sorry you will miss your sister's company but if you are ever in mortal danger, this wand will save you.'

'How can an old burnt bit of wood do that?' I sobbed.

'Believe me,' he said. 'It's magic. To make it work you must first stand on one leg and point it at anyone that's about to harm you. To unleash the magic you must then say the words "Be gone!" Lir looked at me with serious eyes. 'But remember, it is a very powerful spell. You must only use it when your life is threatened.'

As he spoke, a great clamour erupted outside. Angry shouts of 'Quick!' 'This way!' 'He's at the *crannóg*!' could be heard coming from the *ráth* and the noise of running feet and barking dogs filled the night. I saw the bobbing lights of lanterns and heard the splash of oars as boats cast off. The guards at the door, who had been motionless with fear, now sprang forward waving swords at Lir.

'Leave him be,' cried Aobh.

Lir pushed the armed men aside as though they were small children. He gathered Aobh in his cloak and moved towards the door.

'Stay safe, dear Aoife,' Aobh cried from over Lir's shoulder.'

'And don't forget what I said about the magic stick,' called the handsome young man.

I followed them both to say my goodbyes. Outside, by the wall of the *crannóg*, Lir and Aobh briefly hovered above the water before darkness swallowed them up.

***

Bodhbh Dearg was furious when he discovered what had happened.

'My daughter, my beautiful daughter; stolen, by that watery lout,' he cried. I didn't think it prudent to say how willingly Aobh had gone.

My father roared and stamped and bellowed and swore. He cursed Lir from points north and south and east and west.

'May the cat eat that thieving scum and the Darkness eat the cat!' he shouted, shaking his fist at the lake and the sky.

The two *crannóg* guards were sent to work in the pigsty and replaced by four hulking warriors with great, fierce dogs. Orla was banished to the kitchens. In the way of things however, with the passing of time everything calmed and became much as before. Kings and princes still visited seeking my hand, and they were still refused. As the years rolled by, word of my father's obstinacy must have got about for fewer suitors came knocking on the *ráth*'s great gates. It seemed I would live my whole life a lonely prisoner.

I kept the magic stick in my pocket and often pulled it out to dream of Lir. I would kiss the bronze mirror and pretend I was kissing him. It was silly, of course. There was no way I would ever meet the ocean king again. And all the while, the years rolled by, the colour of my hair dimmed and smile-lines deepened into wrinkles on my face.

Early one summer morning, I opened the door of the *crannóg* to view the dawn. The four guards and two dogs lay asleep in an untidy heap on the doorstep. I stepped over men and dogs and none moved.

Bobbing on the lake, close to the island, was a coracle. The little boat lacked mooring ropes yet, as I watched, it remained in one place. This was my chance to escape. Although the coracle had no oars, I climbed in, hunkered down and the boat began to move. It seemed water magic was at work and the only person I knew with this power was Lir. Was my love for him finally going to be rewarded?

The craft skittered across the lake, surged down a river between the wheat fields until it reached the sea. There, despite the pounding waves, the coracle kept going. I have no idea how long we travelled. The journey may have taken a day, or a year,

When, at last, I raised my head, we'd reached a beach with a great castle of rocks at one end. A silver stream led from the castle to the sea. The coracle moved up the stream and into a large cave. Waterfalls sprang from the walls, which were covered with glittering fragments like the scales of a million fish. Trees of coral were hung with glistening pearls and pools winked with sea anemones and jewelled stones. In the middle of all this brilliance sat Lir.

I was so excited to see him again that I jumped from the little coracle and splashed towards him but as I drew close I could see that he was weeping.

'Welcome Lady Aoife, I was expecting you.' He stood up and wiped his tears with the back of one hand. 'It does my heart good to see you at this sad time.'

'Sad?' I said.

'Your sister, my beautiful queen Aobh, died in childbirth. She sacrificed her life giving me sons Fiachra, Aodh and Conn. She also gave me my princess Fionnuala.

I was upset to hear of my sister's death but delighted that Lir had sent for me. He said I comforted him because I looked like Aobh. I was in love with him and within a short time we married. I tried not to notice how he constantly talked of Aobh and how much he had adored her. It made me feel as though I was second best. Although I was happy at first, things slowly changed. So slowly that at the beginning I didn't notice how Lir was spending more and more time with his children and less and less with me. Lir doted on the four and wouldn't hear a word against them though they resented me for not being their mother.

'You're not our mother. You can't tell us what to do,' Fionnuala shouted.

'Aoife's old and ugly as a rotten apple. She looks like this.' Aodh pulled a terrible face.

The twin boys, Fiachra and Conn, stuffed crab shells down the back of my gown and put a dead seagull in my side of the bed. When I fell asleep on the beach they buried me in sand and I almost died from want of air.

It was useless complaining to Lir. He was blind to their hatred of me. 'What endearing little rogues they are,' he'd say and smile.

One afternoon while walking barefoot in the shallows of the sea, I heard the children whispering behind some rocks. I went to put my foot into one of my shoes when a flame-like pain flared up my toes to my ankle and then into my leg: the sting of a jellyfish had been pushed into my shoe. I screamed.

The royal children came towards me, pointing and laughing. Hurt and anger made me desperate. I could take no more of the name calling and bullying. Barely capable of thought beyond a desire for the torment to end, I pulled the magic stick from my pocket and stood on my good leg. 'Be Gone!' I shouted.

A dark, greenish ripple ran over the waves and onto the edge of the beach. A snorting sound and a hail of sparks erupted from the stick. The children were lifted into the air and thrown back on the sand.

Lir came running from the rock castle, clutching his sword.

'You great fool woman!' he shouted. 'See what you've done!'

I bent over each child and put my cheek close to their lips. There was no warm, reassuring breath.

'Can't you see they're dead?' roared Lir. 'And you killed them.'

'I didn't mean any harm,' I cried. 'I only wanted to give them a fright, to make them go away.'

Lir began to howl. Foam poured from his mouth and his eyes flashed red. He grabbed a piece of driftwood and ran in circles, mumbling strange words. A whirlwind of sand began to grow round him. It got bigger, swelling each time he repeated the circle until the whole beach was covered by a seething, murky storm. Helpless, I stumbled about. It seemed magic was happening. 'Please,' I wished. 'Let the children live.'

At last, Lir fell exhausted onto the beach, the wind dropped and the air cleared. The children had gone. There was no sound but the wings of four white swans circling overhead.

'It's them,' Lir peered up. His face was crumpled by agony.

'But why? Why did this happen?'

'I told you my land magic was weak. I brought my little ones back to life, but I could do no more.' Tears slid down Lir's cheeks. 'My children have become swans. Swans, who will be condemned to live for hundreds and hundreds of years on Irish lakes.'

'Can't you transform them back into children?'

'If only I could,' he wailed. 'But no one can alter the magic once it is done. We are all cursed.'

And so it was that I was exiled from Lir's kingdom, condemned to wander forever. Hundreds of years have passed and I have grown very old and tired but I have been denied the peace of death.

Lir followed his swan children to the lakes where they had been forced to live. He died watching his cursed darlings flying over the water singing songs of my cruelty and his heartbreak. I'm told his beautiful palace is now a ruin.

But there is hope. A new wizard has come to Ireland. A man called Patrick who tells strange tales and brings powerful magic. People say Patrick can break spells and save people who are cursed. I'm going to find this wizard and tell him that I made a terrible mistake and I am truly sorry. Folk say Patrick is a kind, good man: if he is, he'll understand. Maybe, just maybe, his new magic will free us all.

Mythological Context: The Children of Lir

Despite the weighty name associated with him (Manannan mac Lir), the mythological figure Lir turns up relatively infrequently in the old Irish literature. In those narratives where he does appear, he's most often referred to as 'Lir of Sídh Fionnachaidh', Sídh Fionnachaidh being a cairn on Deadman's hill (halfway between Armagh and Newry) associated with the Otherworld.

Lir is most famous for his association with the fifteenth century *Oidheadh Chlainne Lir* (The Tragic Fate of the Children of Lir) which tells of his vexation when a competitor – Bodhbh Dearg – is chosen as leader of the Tuath Dé Danann. Lir is appeased only when the latter offers him one of his foster daughters, Aobh, in marriage.

After their union, Aobh bears Lir two sets of twins (first, Aodh and Fionnghuala, then Fiachra and Conn). Unfortunately, while giving birth to the second set of twins, Aodh dies. Bereft and grieving, Lir seeks solace by taking Bodhbh Dearg's second daughter, Aoife, as his new wife.

Although she loves the children at first, Aoife grows to hate them and eventually strikes them at Loch Dairbhreach (in Westmeath) with a magic wand, transforming them into swans. Learning of their fate, Lir transforms Aoife into a demon and curses her to wander the earth forever.

The Children of Lir remain at Loch Dairbhreach for three hundred years, then another three hundred at the Sea of Moyle. After spending a third three hundred years off the coast of Erris in County Mayo, they return to their father's palace at Sídh Fionnachaidh only to find it deserted and in ruins.

At this stage, *Oidheadh Chlainne Lir* states that they return to Inishglory where a Christian missionary Saint Mochaomhóg discovers them and cares for them until the curse runs its course and they're transformed back to human beings. Now withered old men and women, Saint Mochaomhóg baptises them before they die.

The 'Children of Lir' is one of the three great 'tragedy' narratives of ancient Ireland, the other two being 'The Fate of the Sons of Tuirenn' and 'Deirdre of the Sorrows'. It's a tale that pretty much everyone in Ireland is familiar with, primarily from school texts. Because of its popularity in the past, it was relatively common for storytellers to enhance the story by linking the tale to locations their audiences were familiar with. This is why, for example, we also find versions of the tale where the final resting place for the Children of Lir lies beneath a stone near Allihies village on the Beara Peninsula (growing up down there, this was something I assumed to be true throughout my childhood). The role of Saint Mochaomhóg was often replaced by Saint Patrick – depending on who was telling the story.

The story that we all know today is actually believed to have originated from a tale in the Netherlands dating from sometime around the twelfth century. In Ireland, this was the period when Norman knights – some from that particular region – had invaded the country and established a firm foothold. It's believed that the Normans brought this tale over with them and subsequently, a local author incorporated it into local legend.

Coral Atkinson's original and spirited retelling of the ancient legend completely reverses it by recounting the tale from the perspective of Aoife, normally portrayed as the villain in the piece. Portraying the Children of Lir as a bunch of spoiled brats might have been an act of sacrilege in our ancestors' time but provides a wonderful contemporary freshness to the tale.

Brian O'Sullivan

Transit Hours

Marie Gethins

In the grey November twilight Saoirse searched the sea. Flat and black, she struggled to find a ripple in the limpid surface. Below the car park, Rossbeigh strand lay empty. Five years earlier, she and Ian would have been down there walking, watching for seals.

She returned to her battered Golf and drove up the hill to the cottage. They'd bought the place on impulse during a bank holiday weekend. A wreck, the auctioneer had been only too happy to meet them on a Sunday. Ian had called it their "escape hutch" and most weekends they came down from Dublin. At first it had been to put it in some sort of order but later it seemed to be the one place where they were always happiest. Even after the cancer weakened him, Ian had insisted on returning. On the last visit, she'd parked on the rocks above the shore and rolled down the windows so he could taste the salty air. He'd closed his eyes and smiled. She'd squeezed his hand and rubbed a thumb across the back of it, feeling his bones beneath his fragile skin.

Her brother Tomás had stepped in when Ian progressed into the final phase, renting out the cottage, doing maintenance. Since then Tomás kept pushing her to sell it.

Saoirse pulled into the driveway, got out of the car and inserted the key in the front door. The lock opened with a soft click, smoother than she remembered. Inside, she ran a hand along the wall, feeling for the light switch and blinked in the sudden brightness. The cottage smelled of cleaning products and fresh paint.

Returning to the car, she ferried in boxes, her suitcase, a backpack and groceries. The mobile vibrated in her jeans pocket.

'Are you there yet?' Tomás' voice was taut.

'Just arrived. Great job. It looks fabulous.'

'You okay, Saoirse? You shouldn't be there on your own.'

'We've been over this. My therapist thinks it's time.'

'Fuck the therapist.'

'She's really not my type.'

A packet crinkled, lighter clicked. She waited for the sigh of his exhale before continuing.

'Smoking again? Seriously?'

He coughed. '*My* therapist says the odd fag does no harm. Relieves the tension.'

'Fuck the therapist.'

'He's not my type.' Tomás took another drag. "I can be there in a few hours. You shouldn't be alone.'

'I'm okay. I can handle it.'

'Yeah, well. There's no shame in… Ah, you know.'

'Goodnight Tomás.' Saoirse hung up, tossed the mobile onto the couch.

***

She unpacked before walking through the house. Tomás had been thorough – new colour schemes and furniture. The earlier, mismatched pieces scoured from eBay now gone. She paused at the back door where Ian had planned to add another bedroom. For their mythical children.

Two years ago while she was on what the family kindly called her "retreat," Tomás had added a sunroom instead. Curious, she opened the door to survey it: white tile floor, wicker chairs holding bright cushions, a side table with an aromatherapy candle and match box. All it needed was a cat to complete its air of forced cheer. She bit her lower lip.

In the kitchen, Saoirse opened the bottle of Jameson she'd brought along just in case. On the third shot she imagined Tomás asking if it was okay to mix with her meds. On the fifth, she heard Ian's voice admonishing her. Wiping her eyes with the cuff of her shirt, she put the bottle away, collected her mobile and stumbled into bed.

***

The phone alarm woke her just before sunrise. Pulling on wellingtons and a jacket, Saoirse left the cottage, heading down towards the waves. The wind whipped salt spray across her face. Snuggling her chin inside her jacket she breathed deeply, jaw muscles relaxing. Round, flat stones lined the top of the strand: dull purple, grey, and mauve in the dim light of dawn. When she walked on them they shifted and rattled under her feet. A tower of the stones was stacked up on the strand ahead and Saoirse smiled, imagining child-sized hands balancing each addition with care. Despite the strong wind, the tower stood firm.

Stepping off the stones, she continued along the empty beach. Feet sinking in the powdery sand, she angled towards firmer ground at the ocean's edge. Water swirled in and out, occasionally lapping against her boots.

In the distance, she spied a row of what looked like giant teeth – the ribs of an ancient boat wreck. Drawing closer, she circled around the skeletal hull, caught landlocked in sand drifts, curving wood ribs distressed and worn by the tide. She stepped inside, bent down to run her fingers along the rusting metal spine. Splayed and empty, its substance sucked away by a stronger force. Her throat tightened.

Saoirse walked back to the shore. Water, ankle deep, splashed against her feet and then withdrew. Her feet began to sink, the wet sand pulling her. She looked down, tears running the length of her nose, dripping into the surf. She counted seven drops before smearing them across her cheeks and continuing her walk.

When Saoirse came to the end of the strand, she sat on the beach and looked towards the horizon - sky and water a conjoined blue-grey.

'You're not from here, but you know Rossbeigh well.'

Saoirse flinched. A man was sitting beside her, near enough to touch if she stretched out her left hand. Her eyes darted down the strand towards the dunes behind them but she didn't see a second footprint trail. The stranger wore a sueded shirt and moleskin jeans, their dark brown tones matching his longish, wavy hair. His feet were bare.

She eased the mobile out of her pocket, relieved to see the signal bars. 'Aren't you cold?' The words came out before she could think of something better to say. She shuffled a few inches away from him.

The man smiled. 'No, I'm well used to it.' He turned to face her. His eyes were large, deep brown, almost black. 'So, you're back?'

"Ah, yeah.' She looked at him in surprise. 'I've been away for a few years, but I used to come here a lot with my *husband*." As the stress on the last word settled between them she wrapped her arms around her knees, gauging her ability to jump up and sprint in wellingtons.

The man nodded, untroubled by her disquiet. He started to talk, telling her how recent winter storms had changed the area, how the undercurrent had become stronger. 'The Castlemaine beacon washed away in 2011. After one hundred and sixty years.' He sighed then and went quiet.

'This area used to have loads of seals,' said Saoirse. 'Are they all gone?'

'Not all of them,' he laughed.

They sat in silence watching the sun rise, sky and sea splitting the horizon, then the stranger stood up. 'And now I must be off.'

'It's nice meeting you…ah?' Her eyebrows rose.

'Murray. And you are…'

She watched his lips form her name even as she responded. 'Saoirse.' A weight in her abdomen shifted. 'Most people think it's crazy to come to the beach in winter. I guess we're the diehards.'

He inclined his head. 'You'll always find me here in the transit hours.'

'Transit hours?'

'Dawn and dusk. The time of change.'

A sudden squall pelted her with fine sand from the dunes. When she opened her eyes, Murray had disappeared.

***

Back at the cottage she checked her phone. A missed call and three text messages from Tomás. She made coffee and settled into a chair before calling back.

'Tomás, stop panicking.'

'I prefer to consider it as brotherly concern.' His lighter clicked. 'So, you writing?'

'Not yet. Maybe I'll try today.' She picked at a loose thread in her jeans.

'It helped before. I think it would be good.'

'Yeah well, I'll see.' She took a swallow of coffee. 'Listen, I met a guy on the beach this morning.'

'A guy?'

'Some local. Remember that stone beacon? Completely gone now. Washed out during a storm, he told me.'

'Uh-huh. Be careful. Don't let him take advantage.'

'For God's sake. I thought you'd be happy. You know, me mixing with people again.'

Her brother drew on his cigarette and exhaled. Saoirse visualised him: head lowered in thought as he tried to find the right words.

'Listen, I'll talk to you later. Okay?'

Without waiting for an answer, Saoirse hung up, switching the phone to silent. Putting the mobile aside, she moved around the cottage: wiping down counters, fluffing cushions, vacuuming rugs. In the living room, she chewed on a thumb nail while she unzipped her backpack, pulled out a laptop and several books. While the computer was booting up, she flicked through a copy of her last poetry collection, *Alone*. She frowned at the cover: a distraught shadow woman looking at an empty bed. The American edition was worse, its cover reminding her of Edvard Munch's dismal image, *The Scream*.

During Ian's last months, the poems had come out in a rush. Since his death, propelled by caffeine and emotion, she'd spent hours typing but her thoughts were splintered. Now, although she had hundreds of disconnected fragments, she'd been unable to finish a single complete piece since his death.

Opening a new Word file she stared at the white screen, sighed and walked to a window to look out at the strand.

***

At four-thirty, Saoirse hurried down to the beach to watch the sunset. Knee-high white spume collected along the firm sand – a cascade of marshmallow stacks, jiggling in the rising wind. A jogger loped towards her. 'Storm coming,' he called over his shoulder as he ran past.

She arrived at the furthest point of the strand breathless and turned in circles, scanning the beach and sky. Clouds massed, transforming from ash to charcoal as the sun sank into the sea. She walked to the water's edge. Offshore, white caps dotted the surface, rising and falling.

'It will be a rough night. You shouldn't linger.'

Murray was standing next to her, the tide swirling water and froth around his bare feet, soaking the hem of his brown jeans.

She stepped back in alarm. 'Murray! You startled me.'

He smiled.

'So, you live around here?' She hoped her voice sounded casual.

Murray shrugged. 'I have been here always.'

'Hmmm.' Saoirse chewed the side of her cheek and turned her eyes towards the water. 'I've never seen so many white caps.'

'Some believe Niamh and Oisín's white stallion took them from this very beach. All the way from here to Tir na nÓg.'

'Yeah. I wrote a poem about that. Love wasn't enough for him. Oisín left her.'

'Love is always with you and love is stronger than death.'

'Oscar Wilde.' She sighed. 'But you left out:

> Death must be so beautiful.
> To have no yesterday and no to-morrow.
> To forget time, to forget life, to be at peace.

That's the best bit.'

Murray shook his head as though to say that wasn't important. 'The rain will come soon.'

Saoirse walked away, back towards the cottage, eyes narrowed, chin and nose buried in her jacket. As she turned into the driveway, a heavy downpour made her run for the door. Inside, on impulse, she filled the house with light, snapping the switch in every room. Later, wrapped in a blanket, she sat on the couch, sipping tea. A howling wind funnelled down the chimney, rain pelted the windows.

The tea warmed her and she felt her muscles relax, her eyelids drooping. Placing her empty mug on the coffee table beside her mobile, she turned over and fell asleep. Ian's low chuckle and gentle touch filled her dreams until he faded, slipped through her grasp. Saoirse called out after him. 'Ian! Ian!'

A sudden boom rattled the cottage windows, startling her awake. She sat up. Opening her eyes, she tried to focus, saw only black.

A flash of lightning lit the room, followed by a deep rumble of thunder. Saoirse felt her chest tighten and in the next flash, she got to her feet. Arms out straight before her, she reached into the dark, slid her feet along the floor. Two cautious steps and a knee struck the coffee table. Stifling a cry, she rubbed her kneecap.

Another brilliant flash transformed the furniture into crouching animals. Frightened, she made her way to a wall, skimming her hand along its dimpled surface to the sunroom door and then felt her way to the side table.

The small box rattled as she fumbled for a match. Lifting the candle, flame tilted towards the wick, she tried to still her trembling hands. Startled by yet another flash, the flame burned her fingers and she dropped the candle, hearing it strike the floor and roll away in the dark.

'Ian, Ian. It's too bloody hard.'

Saoirse stumbled desperately back through the doorway, bashing against walls and furniture. At the front door, her fingers found the raised metal rectangle of the Yale lock. Turning the bolt, she yanked the door open and ran out into the storm, down towards the strand. When she felt the stones begin to slide beneath her feet, she slowed, followed the slope towards the water. Cold foam brushed against her knees as she walked into the surf.

Pushing against the waves, she waded in until her feet no longer touched sand then flung her arms forward and kicked. Saoirse swam until her muscles burned, her limbs heavy in the sodden jeans and winter sweater. She sank below the churning surface. Water filled her ears, silencing the storm. A stream of air bubbles seeped out of her mouth, slowing until the last popped against her lips. Her chest throbbed. She thought of Tomás searching for the note she didn't write.

Sinking deeper, the water became peaceful. Saoirse imagined a dark hole, the void swallowing her.

Seaweed brushed against her hands. Something bumped against her back and then nosed under her arm, halting her descent. Instead, she was propelled upwards. Breaking the surface, her natural instincts suppressed her intent. She struggled for air. A wave crashed over her head, filling her mouth with salt water. Saoirse steadied herself against the body next to her. Stiff whiskers nuzzled her cheek and she caught a glimpse of a pair of large, brown eyes.

Buoyed by the harbour seal under her arm, they moved back towards land. Ripples streamed past. Her feet began to snag along rocks, shells and sand. Nudged out of the water by the seal, she lay limp on the beach. Rain splattered exposed skin. The tide swirled around her ankles. Her mind drifted until a pair of hands grabbed her shoulders and dragged her up the slope. Pulling her onto her knees, a forearm slid around her waist, one hand held back her hair.

'Release, Saoirse, release.'

The arm pressed against her stomach. She retched several times, the clear fluid absorbed by the sand. A bare male foot – calloused and scarred - stood alongside the fading puddle.

'I'm sorry,' she said. 'I'm sorry.'

Murray grunted in response and carried her into the dunes. At the entrance to a rocky shelter, he placed her on a bed of sea grass. She watched him reach behind a rock and unroll a dappled brown pelt, smoothing it out on the shelter floor then he knelt down beside her. His wet hair hung loose around his face, dripping onto his shoulders. She tried to speak through chattering teeth, but he hushed her, rubbing a finger across her lips and shaking his head. She didn't resist as he peeled her out of her sodden clothes.

Lying on the pelt, she sank her fingers into the deep pile. He pulled her close against him. Skin to skin, his warmth calmed her shivering. Feeling the rub of his nose along her neck, Saoirse stiffened.

'I can't. I can't do this.' She tried to roll away.

Murray loosened his grip, but remained beside her.

Saoirse turned to face him, drawn by the smell of salt and seaweed. 'I know what you are, what you seem to be,' she said. 'But you can't be real.'

He shrugged. 'Then dream,' he answered. 'Dream with me for a little while.'

'Ian … Ian used to say "Dreams are what makes life tolerable". But … You probably knew that since you seem to know everything about Ian and me.'

Murray smiled and stroked her back.

Later he woke Saoirse from an untroubled sleep. Outside the shelter, a hazy purple light signalled the incoming dawn. Murray pointed to the patch of brightening sky. 'I must leave,' he said.

Gathering up the pelt, he waved at her then turned and made his way out of the dunes.

In silence, she dressed in her damp clothing and went down the beach, walked along firm sand and turned up the road towards the cottage.

The door stood open when she returned. The welcome mat squelched beneath her feet. She switched the lights off and straightened the disarray before she turned on her laptop and began to type

Mythological Context: The Male Selkie

As with the earlier 'A Mainland Mansie Meur', Marie Gethins' tale tells involves a folklore creature – the Selkie – helping a human being through a difficult period of grieving for a loved one although, on this occasion, in a much more direct manner. This particular story involves the presence of a male selkie (a derivation of the previously mentioned *Fear Mara*).

Once again, most of the folklore with respect to the male selkie seems to originate predominantly from the romanticised tales of Walter Traill Dennison in his 'Orcadain Sketches' and other writings. According to Denniston, the selkie-men were very handsome in their human state and had great seductive appeal for mortal women. Denniston's writing also outlined a ritual that was to be followed when a mortal woman sought contact with a selkie-man. This involved walking towards the seashore at high tide and shedding seven tears into the sea, an action that has great ramifications for the wounded protagonist in this story.

Growing up in West Cork, I spent many days sitting by the water's edge and often raised my eyes to find a seal head poking out of the water just offshore, observing me with interest. For anyone who's lived by the sea in Ireland and the British Isles, the possibility of transition from seal to human actually sounds eminently believable.

Brian O'Sullivan

The Authors

Sighle Meehan

Winner of *Poems for Patients* and *Goldsmith Poetry* (2014), runner-up in *Fish Poetry* (2014), shortlisted three times in the *Over the Edge*, shortlisted in *Cúirt*, and longlisted in the Desmond O'Grady poetry competitions. Her poems have been published in *Fish, Crannóg, The Stinging Fly, Boyne Berries, Skylight 47* and the *Galway Advertiser*. Her full-length, bi-lingual play, *Maum*, was produced by *Taibhdhearc na Gaillimhe* for the Galway International Arts Festival in 2015. This is Sighle's first attempt at short story telling.

Sheelagh Russell Brown

Sheelagh Russell Brown is the descendant (on her mother's side) of an Orkneyman who came to Drummondville, Quebec and then to New Brunswick, Canada, in the late nineteenth century. She is descended from Irish immigrants on her father's side. Her story is very loosely based on her Orkney great-grandfather.

Having taught for seven years in the Czech Republic, Sheelagh has been (for the past thirteen years) a lecturer in English literature at Saint Mary's University in Halifax, NS. She has published papers on the "shadow" of Havel in Beckett's play "Catastrophe," on memories of the Holocaust among European Roma, and on the use of wordplay in Hopkins's "Dark Sonnets." Her field of specialization is nineteenth- and twentieth- century British and European literature.

Marc McEntegart

Marc McEntegart is a Dublin-based writer and editor whose work is largely focussed on the games industry. His fondness for Celtic mythology comes from long summer drives in the passenger seat beside his grandfather.

When not writing or playing videogames, he spends his time playing capoeira.

Coral Atkinson

Choiréil Mac Aidicin /Coral Atkinson was born in Dublin, Ireland and came to New Zealand with her family as a girl. She is a graduate of the University of Canterbury and has worked as a teacher, educational journalist and in book publishing. She has also tutored publishing and creative writing. She held the Ursula Bethell Residency in Creative Writing at the University of Canterbury in 2015.

Coral has had fiction published in New Zealand, Ireland and England and won and been short-listed for a number of short story competitions. In 2005 her first historical novel, The Love Apple, appeared and was followed in 2006 by The Paua Tower; both published by Random House NZ. She co-authored the self-help book, Recycled People: Forming New Relationships in Mid-Life, Shoal Bay Press, 2000. Her picture book on New Zealand history, Magic Eyes; I Spy New Zealand History, was published by Reed in 2006. Her junior historical novel, Copper Top, published by Dancing Tuatara appeared in 2009. Her most recent adult historical novel, Passing Through, was released in 2014. It is soon to be serialised on Radio New Zealand.

Coral has also published various articles, essays and educational texts. She lives in Governors Bay on Banks Peninsula. She enjoys gardening and is an animal lover.

Marie Gethins

Marie Gethins' creative writing has featured in the 2014 and 2015 National Flash Fiction Day Anthologies, Flash: The International Short-Short Story Magazine, Litro, NANO, The Lonely Crowd, Wales Arts Review, The Incubator, Circa, Words with JAM,

Firewords Quarterly and others. She won or placed in The Short Story, Tethered by Letters flash, Flash500, Dromineer Literary Festival, The New Writer Microfiction, Prick of the Spindle and 99fiction.net. Other pieces have been listed in the Bristol Short Story Prize, Fish Short Story/Flash/Memoir, James Plunkett Award, Listowel Writers Week Originals, Inktears, RTE/Penguin, Molotav Cocktail, Lightship, Doris Gooderson, Over the Edge and WOW! Award competitions. Marie is a Pushcart and Best of the Short Fictions Nominee. Awarded B.A.'s in English Literature and Dramatic Art/Dance from U.C. Berkeley, she is working on her Master of Studies in Creative Writing at the University of Oxford. She lives with her family in Cork, Ireland.

Brian O'Sullivan

Brian O'Sullivan was born in county Cork, Ireland. On completing a degree at University College Cork, he went on to travel extensively. He is now based in New Zealand where he runs Irish Imbas Books with his partner and family but returns to Ireland on a regular basis. He writes weekly articles on Irish mythology and folklore, aspects of Irish culture and his own writing at the **Irish Imbas Books** website.

Brian writes fiction that incorporates strong elements of Irish culture, language, history and mythology. These include literary short stories, mystery thrillers (The Beara Trilogy) and a contemporary version of the Fionn mac Cumhaill/ Fenian legends (The Fionn mac Cumhaill Series).

The Celtic Mythology Short Story Competition

The **Celtic Mythology Short Story Competition** is an initiative established by Irish Imbas Books to promote the writing of contemporary Celtic culture-based stories and to encourage a more accurate understanding of that culture.

This book, the **Irish Imbas: Celtic Mythology Short Story Collection 2016** is the first output from this initiative. It is hoped to repeat the competition and the publication of appropriate stories on an annual basis.

Full details for this competition can be found at the Irish Imbas Books website **irishimbasbooks.com**.

Prizes: include:

First Prize: $500 and story published in the next Irish Imbas Celtic Mythology Collection
Second prize: $250 and story published in the next Irish Imbas Celtic Mythology Collection
Third prize: $100 and story published in the next Irish Imbas Celtic Mythology Collection

Any kind of fiction short story can be submitted (action, romance, drama, humour etc.) as long as they meet the following criteria:

- Celtic mythology forms a fundamental element of the story (i.e. the characters can be characters from Celtic mythology, the action can take place in a mythological location, mythological concepts can be used etc.)
- Any Celtic folklore or mythological reference used in the story should be as authentic and as correct as possible

- The story should have a compelling theme, engaging characters etc.

Submissions for the next competition will be accepted from June 2016.

Another Complimentary Book

To celebrate its two years of operation, Irish Imbas Books are offering a **complimentary copy** of **Fionn Defence of Ráth Bládmha** for a limited period. Copies of this novel can be obtained by signing up for the monthly newsletter at: **irishimbasbooks.com**.

Fionn: Defence of Ráth Bládhma:
[The Fionn mac Cumhaill Series: Book 1]

Ireland: 192 A.D. A time of strife and treachery. Political ambition and inter-tribal conflict has set the country on edge, testing the strength of long-established alliances.

Following their victory at the battle of Cnucha, Clann Morna are hungry for power. Meanwhile, a mysterious war party roams the 'Great Wild' and a ruthless magician is intent on murder.

In the secluded valley of Glenn Ceoch, disgraced druidess Bodhmhall and her lover Liath Luachra have successfully avoided the bloodshed for many years. Now, the arrival of a pregnant refugee threatens the peace they have created together. The odds are overwhelming and death stalks on every side.

Based on the ancient Irish Fenian Cycle texts, the Fionn mac Cumhaill Series recounts the fascinating and pulse-pounding tale of the birth and adventures of Ireland's greatest hero, Fionn mac Cumhaill.

A sample of what the reviewers say:

"An Ireland of centuries ago, threaded through with myth and magic, but very 'real' for all that. Dark and at times very violent, it is balanced by affirming friendships and relationships, and a very strong female cast."

"The violence and brutality of ancient Ireland presented on a very human scale, with real characters of depth and substance."

"If you're sick of elves, chivalrous knights and arcane quests like me, this is probably the most exciting and refreshing book you'll read in a long time. Five stars!"

'Powerful female characters are all too rare in literature. The druidess Bodhmhall, and her lover the warrior Liath Luachra will inspire current and future generations of women. O'Sullivan keeps a cracking pace in this, the first of his Fionn mac Cumhaill series.'

Other Books from Irish Imbas Books:

See the Irish Imbas Books website and blog at irishimbasbooks.com for contact details and updates on new and upcoming titles.

Beara: Dark Legends

[The Beara Trilogy – Book 1]

Nobody knows much about reclusive historian Muiris (Mos) O'Súilleabháin except that he doesn't share his secrets freely. Mos, however, has a *"sixth sense for history, a unique talent for finding lost things"*.

Reluctantly lured from seclusion, despite his own misgivings, Mos is hired to locate the final resting place of legendary Irish hero, Fionn mac Cumhaill. Confronted by a thousand year old mystery, the distractions of a beguiling circus performer and a lethal competitor, Mos must draw on his knowledge of Gaelic lore to defy his enemies and survive his own family history in Beara.

Beara: Dark Legends is the first in a trilogy of unforgettable Irish thrillers. Propulsive, atmospheric and darkly humorous, *Dark Legends* introduces an Irish hero like you've never seen before. Nothing you thought you knew about Ireland will ever be the same again.

A sample of what the reviewers say:

"A great tale with all the elements of a "Who dunnit" all woven into modern and ancient Irish history and mythology."

"Fantastic book - couldn't put it down. A 'MUST' read! original Irish thriller, historical novel, mystery novel, best book I've read in years."

"O'Sullivan has done an amazing job of introducing a culture that many would say is dying and using it as the basis for a unique and exciting thriller. I think I've learned more about Irish history and the Irish language in this one book than I have in many years of school and television, without it once feeling forced or jaded."

"A great mixture of a strong story and strong characters, dark (some very dark) themes and wonderfully evocative descriptions of the wild Irish landscape, interspersed with ancient Irish lore running throughout the book."

"Excellent story, very well thought out, many twists and turns that weren't expected. Thoroughly enjoyed the main character Mos and his no nonsense-take no crap attitude to life, he says what most of us often probably think but are too polite to say, highly entertaining!"

"O'Sullivan's cast of international characters enliven this tale of archaeological intrigue, magic, murder and sex, set mainly in West Cork, Ireland. Dual story lines, across different time zones, reveal secrets of Irish spirituality, ancient lore and language."

The Irish Muse and Other Stories

This intriguing collection of stories puts an original twist on foreign and familiar territory. Merging the passion and wit of Irish storytelling with the down-to-earth flavour of other international locations around the world, these stories include:

- a ringmaster's daughter who is too implausible to be true — despite all the evidence to the contrary
- an ageing nightclub gigolo in one last desperate bid to best a younger rival
- an Irish consultant whose uncomplicated affair with a public service colleague proves anything but
- an Irish career woman in London stalked by a mysterious figure from her past

A sample of what the reviewers say:

"This is a delightful book of short stories by new author Brian O'Sullivan. The stories, which are set both in Ireland and New Zealand, are a mixture of tender whimsy and sharp irony, in a collection that will delight."

"It's fiction tinged with a bit of real life experience, set in Wellington, Ireland and France amongst other places. The stories range from chance romantic encounters in a small Irish town and haunting tales of tragic personal loss to bizarre encounters between a consultant and a career woman in Wellington and one man's attempt to get to the bottom of his internet service woes. The finale was a thought-provoking tale that upended my perception of indigenous people's land grievances, oddly entitled 'Morris Dancing' It's said that you can't judge a book by its cover. Au contraire, I liked the look of O'Sullivan's book and the content proved to be good."

"This is a delightful book of short stories by new author Brian O'Sullivan. The stories, which are set both in Ireland and New Zealand, are a mixture of tender whimsy and sharp irony, in a collection that will delight. It has all the clichés of Ireland, but a modern tone that interweaves the magical and realistic in a wonderful, whimsical mix."

Liath Luachra: The Grey One

Ireland: 188 A.D. A land of tribal affiliations, secret alliances and treacherous rivalries.

Youthful woman warrior Liath Luachra has survived two brutal years fighting with mercenary war party "The Friendly Ones" but now the winds are shifting.

Dispatched on a murderous errand where nothing is as it seems, she must survive a group of treacherous comrades, the unwanted advances of her battle leader and a personal history that might be her own.

Clanless and friendless, she can count on nothing but her wits, her fighting skills and her natural ferocity to see her through.

Woman warrior, survivor, killer and future guardian to Irish hero Fionn mac Cumhaill – this is her story.

A sample of what the reviewers say:

"In the legends of Fionn mac Cumhaill, Liath Luachra is an intriguing name with minimal context but in Brian O'Sullivan's adaptions she becomes a most fascinating and formidable character in her own right. Her backstory is a great read; brigands and bloodshed, second-guessings and double-crossings. This is an Ancient Ireland that is entrancing and savage, much like Liath Luachra herself."

"I re-immersed myself in the very believable world the author creates, and couldn't put the book down until I had finished it. It shed so much light on the character of Liath - her grim experiences and her strength in the face of adversity. I am now going back to reread the other books, which I am sure will be all the richer for a greater understanding of Liath. You don't often come across such a compelling hero(ine), written with such depth and understanding."

"This is a fast paced traverse through bush trails and battles with a female heroine who is commanding and fascinating."

"As always, the plotting is riveting – full of twists and turns – and the action is full on, hell for leather. If you like Games of Thrones style dramas with a strong splash of Celtic culture, this is a book you'll enjoy!"

'Once again Brian O'Sullivan has created a thrilling historical drama. Liath Luachra provides strong ties to his other books (although each also stands alone very well). I think it's the depth of knowledge and research that adds the extra dimension that appeals to me but I really liked the fast pace, the developed relationships and the writing style.

If you'd like to receive our monthly newsletter on future books and audio (some not available through the larger ebookstores), elements of Irish mythology, folklore, culture and the creative process we use, please feel free to sign up at **irishimbasbooks.com**.

Printed in Great Britain
by Amazon